My Calm-Down Books

I CAN CREATE

Caitie McAneney

PowerKiDS press

PK Beginners

I feel sad!
I want to cry.

I feel mad!
I want to yell.

Big feelings are hard.
What can I do?

I can create.
That means making
something new.

I can make a picture.
It shows how I feel.

I can write a story.
It tells how I feel.

I can make a song.
I turn feelings
into music.

I can make
a new dance.
It helps to move
my body!

It is fun
to create things.
Time flies by.

Now I feel calm.
Calm means peaceful.

I used my big feelings.
I am proud
of what I made!

Published in 2024 by The Rosen Publishing Group, Inc.
2544 Clinton St, Buffalo, NY 14224

First Edition

Editor: Caitie McAneney
Book Design: Rachel Rising

Photo Credits: Cover, p. 1 A Lot Of People/Shutterstock.com; p. 3 Art_Photo/Shutterstock.com; p. 5 Pressmaster/Shutterstock.com; p. 7 Luis Molinero/Shuttestock.com; p. 9 ARTEM VOROPAI/Shutterstock.com; p. 11 Prostock-studio/Shutterstock.com; p. 13 balanser/Shutterstock.com; p. 15 ANURAK PONGPATIMET/Shutterstock.com; p. 17 BearFotos/Shutterstock.com; p. 19 wavebreakmedia/Shutterstock.com; p. 21 fizkes/Shutterstock.com; p. 23 all_about_people/Shutterstock.com.

Cataloging-in-Publication Data
Names: McAneney, Caitie.
Title: I can create / Caitie McAneney.
Description: New York : Powerkids Press, 2024. | Series: My calm-down books
Identifiers: ISBN 9781642824940 (pbk.) | ISBN 9781642824957 (library bound) | ISBN 9781642824964 (ebook)
Subjects: LCSH: Emotions in children--Juvenile literature. | Art therapy for children--Juvenile literature. | Creative ability in children--Juvenile literature.
Classification: LCC BF723.E6 M45 2024 | DDC 155.4'124--dc23

Manufactured in the United States of America

CPSIA Compliance Information: Batch #CSPK24. For further information contact Rosen Publishing at 1-800-237-9932.